THIS WALKER BOOK BELONGS TO:

_____

_____

_____

_____

For my wonderful grandmother
A. H.

For Birdie, who showed me
that the beauty of the home is a wellspring of life
C. A. N.

Published 2001 by Walker Books Ltd
87 Vauxhall Walk, London SE11 5HJ

This edition published 2002

2 4 6 8 10 9 7 5 3 1

Text © 2001 Amy Hest
Illustrations © 2001 Claire A. Nivola

This book has been typeset in Centaur

Printed in Hong Kong

British Library Cataloguing in Publication Data:
a catalogue record for this book is available from the British Library

ISBN 0-7445-9426-X

The Friday Nights of Nana

Amy Hest

illustrated by Claire A. Nivola

WALKER BOOKS
AND SUBSIDIARIES
LONDON • BOSTON • SYDNEY

The Friday nights of Nana begin early Friday morning in her kitchen, and we are eating bread with sweet peach jam, which is her favourite and mine. Nana sips tea and the tea is too hot and she blows in the old china cup, making ripples.

"Today I have no school!" I sing. "Lucky me!"

"Today you have no school!" she answers. "Lucky ME!"

"Now tell about tonight," I say.

"The family is coming! The family is coming for Sabbath and we have work to do!" Nana zips inside to make the bed and tidy the rooms. I'm in charge of fluffing pillows.

Nana washes the good china and irons all the wrinkles
in her lace tablecloth. I fold napkins with lace borders.

She checks for missing buttons on her Sabbath dress,
navy blue with a round white collar and white cuffs, too.

"Is it time to make pie?" I ask.

"Soon, Jennie."

I polish, and polish, two candleholders.

"Now is it time?"

"Now," Nana says, rolling out dough, and I sweeten apples for the pie with sugar. Then she braids challah breads, and tucks them in the oven.

At noon we eat sandwiches in the park near the river.
There's cocoa, too, in teacups.

The sky is grey and wind blows off the river, blowing our hair straight up, and we dance to keep warm, wearing ponchos and mittens.

Afterwards, we hold hands on city streets, looking for
violet-coloured flowers, which are Nana's favourites and mine.
The flower man wraps them up in green wrapping-paper.

"Why, thank you," says Nana.

And, "Thank you," I say, skipping along with my flowers.

When we get back to Nana's, we put them in a tall vase with water.

"Is it time to get dressed?" I ask.

"Soon, Jennie."

By late afternoon the house is all scrubbed, barley soup simmers and the challahs cool off. Chicken is baking, and also the potatoes.

"Now is it time?"

"Now," Nana says, and we get dressed up in dresses that are both navy blue. Our shoes are blue, too. Nana puts on lipstick, watching her lips in the mirror.

We set the table, counting silver and soup bowls, glasses that sparkle. Nana pokes the chicken to see if it is tender.

Outside it is getting dark. "Look, Nana, snow!"

The doorbell rings and the family pours in, hugging
Nana. They hug me, too, especially my parents, and I
tickle my baby brother, Lewis, in his baby-bunny sleeper.

The doorbell rings and more family pours in! The
uncles, aunts and cousins. Everyone talks at the same
time, kicking off boots, dropping coats on chairs.
You can smell my pie in the oven.

"Is it time?" I ask.

"Now," Nana says, and finally it's the best time. Nana is lighting candles and our dresses are touching and she is whispering Sabbath prayers and no one makes a peep. Not even Lewis.

Soon we are munching the challahs and passing soup
bowls, and everyone talks at the same time at the long
dining table.

Outside, the wind howls. Snow whips up in great
white swirls.

But here inside, the candles flicker.
A Sabbath song is in the air. It's time for
pie and we're all here together on the
Friday nights of Nana.

❖ ❖

AMY HEST says of *The Friday Nights of Nana*,
"I remember lighting Friday night candles with my
grandmother when I was younger. It is a lovely tradition."
She adds, "Time with a grandparent is very special and
children remember it always."

Amy is the author of many books for young readers,
including *When Jessie Came Across the Sea*, illustrated by
P. J. Lynch and Winner of the Kate Greenaway Medal; the
award-winning Baby Duck books, illustrated by Jill Barton;
and *Kiss Goodnight, Sam* and *Don't You Feel Well, Sam?*,
illustrated by Anita Jeram.

CLAIRE A. NIVOLA is a painter, sculptor and illustrator.
Among her books are *Elisabeth*, which she also wrote,
and *The Mouse of Amherst* by Elizabeth Spires. Claire
fills her pictures with a wealth of wonderful detail inspired
by the furnishings and objects around her. In fact, she says,
"The rooms in *The Friday Nights of Nana* are a composite
of the various places I have lived in throughout my life."
She lives in Massachusetts, USA with her husband,
son and daughter.